CW01456468

A Short Touch of Bristol

by
Carbaretta Bartland

Third Edition
© 2020 Carbaretta Bartland. All rights reserved.

This book or any portion thereof may not be reproduced or used in any manner whatsoever without the express written permission of the publisher except for the use of brief quotations in a book review.

All characters and other entities appearing in this work are fictitious. Any resemblance to real persons, dead or alive, or other real-life entities, past or present, is purely coincidental.

Fanybedwell Press
The Old Rectory
Cockshute Lane
Bell End
Worcestershire
WR69 4BJ

For friends of Carbaretta everywhere

"Harder, Muriel, harder!" echoed the booming voice of Mr Derek Beavis down the stone tower staircase. "Tighten your grip and give it a good strong flick of the wrist, or you'll never get it up!"

Sally sighed and continued her iron-footed trudge to the top of the spiral steps for yet another lacklustre practice. If Muriel was there, there would be ten minutes of ringing up, fifteen minutes of Plain Bob troubles, and the rest of the evening filled with veiled bitching about the flower arranging rota whilst doling out the Quality Street. *Oh well.... Grin and bear it as usual...* By the time she stepped into the ringing room, Muriel looked utterly exhausted, whilst Mr Beavis was puce-cheeked with the vigorous effort of miming the required action to no discernible effect. Quite why Muriel could never get the treble up was a total mystery. Admittedly, it was not well hung; and yes, it hadn't been lubricated properly in years. But still, it really wasn't that big, and Mr Beavis had got an expert in to take a look at it, such that it was at the very least comfortable to handle.

"Look, Muriel," he insisted. "It's going floppy. Give it a good tug or it's never going to happen!"

"I don't know what to do!" wailed Muriel.

"Take another couple of inches!" insisted Derek. "Show it that you mean business!"

Sally shoved two years of *Ringing World* back copies along the bench and plonked herself down unnoticed. What with The Archers currently being in the throes of a particularly gripping suicide bomber plotline, nobody else had turned up yet, apart from Mike, who was putting his Coxwell Place into the simulator ready for Thursday's tied session, and Hazel, who sat hunched in her dungarees over a frayed bell rope with a needle and thread. Hazel was particularly adept at whipping and was clearly relishing every moment of her new role as Tower Captain. Judging by the state of her dungarees, she must have been upstairs greasing nipples all afternoon. At least she was useful on the technical side. Where actual ringing was concerned, she was a liability, if anything. She had even acquired the nickname of Hurricane Hazel, thanks to her tendency to turn up when you were least expecting her and completely destroy Glasgow, London and Cambridge. Happy to have a few spare moments whilst the others were gainfully occupied, Sally seized the opportunity to pop out her Bristol in a last-ditch effort to sort out the front end once and for all.

So absorbed was she in trying to rectify the parlous state of her Bristol, that by the time she looked up from her studies, the population of the ringing room had tripled and, with an almost unprecedented delay of a mere twelve minutes, the practice was threatening to get underway.

"Take hold of the nearest one," said Mr Beavis, "and let's get the rest of them up together."

Sally grabbed the Four and waited, coils in hand, while Phyllis and Veronica thrashed out the finer details of the chrysanthemum situation in readiness for Sunday's special service.

"Look to!" spluttered Mr Beavis.

Phyllis and Veronica moved on to the perennial issue of where the spare blocks of oasis were stored.

"Look to!" spluttered Mr Beavis at a fractionally raised decibel level.

Phyllis and Veronica huddled together so as not to be overheard discussing Thelma's continued failure to wash out the vases properly and Fenella's 'artistic' approach to the pew sheet.

"Look to!" shouted Mr Beavis, using his best scary

Geography teacher voice, the one that hadn't had to be used since the WI Bake Sale food poisoning incident had been the talk of the tower.

Reluctantly, Phyllis and Veronica looked to. They seemed somewhat aggrieved that, at a bell-ringing practice, they were being expected to get on with some bell-ringing.

"Here's one!"

And off they went, ringing up with all the precision and crispness of a squid trying to negotiate its way out of a bathful of sherry trifle. Sally exchanged knowing glances with Crispin, who was gamely attempting to keep things in some semblance of order with his steady handling of the tenor. Sally was fond of Crispin, who had worked hard to make progress since starting to ring the previous summer, in spite of his rather patchy attendance. (He had been preoccupied with his mother's undercarriage for most of the autumn and had also missed last week, when the pair of them went to the first night of *Cats on Ice* at the Wembley Arena to celebrate the successful shoring up of her pelvic floor.) Between rings, Sally liked to sit with Crispin and help him with the theory of his Rounds and Call Changes. He was perfectly comfortable with getting into and out of Queens - a natural, even - but for the time being, Tittums were well and truly off the menu.

What about my needs, though? thought Sally, as the bells started to slow and nearly, ever so nearly, came into some semblance of rounds, albeit with the customary assortment of crashing at the front, at the back and in the middle for good measure. *I'm doing a whole load of helping, but who's helping me? I need a man who caters to my every need. A man who can unblock my cinques once and for all.* Nobody had ever looked at her front work. Nobody had looked at her back work, for that matter. She had just had to do it all by herself, and quite how anyone is supposed to know whether or not they are doing it properly if there's nobody there to offer a guiding hand, she had no idea.

As for finding anyone else solid enough to actually ring with, it was a desert out there. Mike was a good ringer, admittedly, but he was obsessed with obscure methods that nobody else would ever bother to try. He once persuaded her to drive all the way to Kidderminster for a quarter of Lickey End Treble Bob Major but it was doomed to failure before it even started and went pear-shaped after just three leads. Since then, she had generally avoided his advances and had already told him after Sunday Service ringing that she was just not interested in getting Onacock Treble Bob Major on Friday morning at Wistanstow.

Sally just wanted to make places with somebody who knew what he was doing, and feel safe, safe in the knowledge that it would all come to a satisfying conclusion, not just collapse after two minutes in a damp squib of regrets and recriminations. She hadn't had a sniff of a successful quarter at St James the Dismembered in months, let alone a full peal. All she ever got was Mr Beavis' unadventurous, disappointing touches, touches which did nothing for her and invariably left her unaffected. She longed for the touch of a real man, a touch that would really hit the spot and force her to respond to the challenge. A touch that would linger. But who in this whole wide Guild could provide such a touch?

And then, out of nowhere, there he was!

"Hi, everyone," he said. "I'm Robert."

"Hello!" said everyone, pretty much in unison, which was the first thing that they had managed to do as a coherent band all evening.

"I've just moved to Shropshire now that my international rugby playing days are sadly behind me..."

International rugby? thought Sally. *That explains the legs. And clearly not one of the ones that has to go in the scrum, as I'm looking at his ears and they're reminding me of tropical flowers, as opposed to Spam.*

"I thought it would be a good opportunity to get

back into ringing. See if I can finally get round to joining the 5000 Peals club. Captaining England has rather got in the way of late."

"I'm Sally." She reached out to shake his hand, almost trembling with the thrill of actually feeling the concrete physicality of this otherwise godlike figure.

"What do you ring, Sally?" asked Robert.

"Mainly Stedman, but I'm keen to have a go at Cockshute Bob."

"What a coincidence! I've just been working on my Cockshute so I'm sure we can get it to go."

"You'll have to call me Observation, though..." interrupted Sally coyly.

"Whatever you say, Observation. And you can call me Bob."

"Bob." *I like that,* thought Sally. *It has a certain ring to it. A certain mystery. It sounds like the kind of name that keeps popping up out of the blue and means something different every time you hear it.* She fixed him with her gaze and repeated his name to ensure that she would never forget it: "Bob."

Then, glancing down, she noticed his left hand. No

ring!

"Single, Bob?"

"Single," Bob nodded. And then, looking her straight in the eyes with an unwavering focus, he hammered it home: "Single."

Single... mused Sally in rapture. *Bob: single!* The rapidly accelerating thud of her heart was almost audible.

Steadying herself with all the power she could muster, Sally changed the subject. "I fear it won't be all that easy to get a band together for Cockshute in this neck of the woods."

"Leave that to me," said Robert with a reassuring nonchalance. "I'll make it the climax of a one-day tour of invitation-only towers in mid-Shropshire: Worfield, Cound, Acton Burnell..."

"Willey?" suggested Sally. "Nice light five. Bit on the small side but lovely and smooth, so I'm told. I've been dying to grab Willey for years."

"Hmm... five bells..." mused Robert. "Cockshute without a cover, perhaps? Do you want to risk it?"

"Nothing ventured, nothing gained," she assured him, with a twinkle in her eye.

"Right," said Mr Beavis. "Crispin wants to get his hands on the tenor, so time for some Plain Bob Doubles. Sally, if you wouldn't mind giving us a sturdy treble, that would be lovely. Fill in, everyone else, please."

"I'll observe for now, if that's OK," said Robert.

"By all means," said Mr Beavis. "If you can hover around the Two and keep Muriel going, that would be much appreciated. You won't let it drop now you're in expert hands, will you, Muriel?"

"No, Derek," replied Muriel. "I'm going to keep it up if it's the last thing I do!"

Robert was secretly thrilled to have been given the task of attending to Muriel's needs, as it gave him the opportunity to stand behind Sally and absorb her captivating aroma. She smelt of honey blossom, jasmine, sandalwood and small furry animals. (Clean small furry animals like prize chinchillas, not beavers or anything like that.) He could imagine her spending her afternoons in a cottage garden, combing the tangles out of freshly shampooed golden hamsters, all the while muttering *Run in... Double Dodge... Lead full...* to herself in a reverie of Cornwall front-work.

"Look to. Treble's going. She's gone."

Sally plunged herself into the task at hand, trying hard not to lose herself in the bewildering closeness of Robert, whose entire aura seemed to envelop her. *Concentrate,* she thought with intensity. *This must be perfect. He must see no failings in my plain hunt.* The band got through the first lead without a hitch and - there was no denying it - Sally's striking was striking.

"God, I need your hunt," whispered Robert in her ear.

"Stand!" called Derek. (Phyllis had missed the dodge and was now rubbing up against his Five with no realistic hope of escape or rectification.)

Had Sally misheard him?

"I need your hunt," he whispered again in her ear.

"Really?" she replied, not daring to turn around and look at him, for fear of revealing her blushes.

"Yes, really. We have a peal of Double Norwich Caters coming up and our Treble's just dropped out. Someone was a bit too heavy-handed with his mini-ring at an open-air festival in Bromsgrove. He has to go and get it tightened up as a matter of urgency."

"Gosh, I'm not sure if I can handle the full Double

Norwich just yet."

"Oh, poppycock! Of course you can! Anyone with a perfect hunt like yours can handle Double Norwich!"

"But for three whole hours? Do you really think it will hold out? I've never done it for that long before."

"You'll be fine. I'll be on the Two, so you can run out with me and lie at the back for a few leads. Once you've got to grips with that, we can really get going and as long as you keep your nerve and really knuckle down for the long haul, we'll get you over the line. I'm not going to lie to you. It's going to be long and it's going to be hard. But I have faith in you. And we'll get through it together."

"But are you sure I won't let you down?" asked Sally nervously. "I mean, just wait until you see Mike hunt."

"Mike? I wouldn't have thought it to look at him."

"Oh yes," said Sally with conviction. "You're really in for a treat when you see Mike hunt. Beautifully smooth and even at the front and the back…"

"And no clipping?"

"Of course not," said Sally. "Mike hunts without even the slightest flaw…"

"Well, that's good to know, but nevertheless…" said Robert, pausing to give her a meaningful, lasting gaze. "…fate has brought us together and it's you, Sally, and your hunt that I want to keep a steady hold of my Double Norwich."

Out of nowhere, a voice from the other side of the tower pierced the bubble of that perfect moment.

"Oh well, never mind…" said Mr Beavis. "We'll try that again later. Now, Veronica, can we have a look at your Reverse Canterbury Pleasure Place?"

"Oh dear, Derek. I'm afraid it's a bit rusty."

"Not to worry, Vee. Not to worry. Just a plain course to start with. We'll soon whip it into shape. If we all just scrutinise it for a couple of minutes and memorise the circle of work, I'm sure none of us will forget it."

"Very well, but I don't hold out much hope," said Veronica, pessimistically. "I'm still a bit loose at the back."

Veronica is loose everywhere, let alone the back, thought Sally. Not that many of the others were much better. Put Veronica, Phyllis and Muriel all into Rounds and Call Changes together and it was a recipe for late leads and lumpy Tittums all round.

"Do you need a box?" Sally asked Robert.

Do I ever... he thought, but replied: "No, thanks. If anything, it'll be too long and I'll probably have to put a knot in it."

And so they got underway, this time with Robert on the Five and Sally on the Two. In spite of the ill omens, it actually bumped along quite nicely, with Robert and Sally making particularly tidy places every time they met and Crispin handling the tenor with an impressive level of focus and tenacity. (He wasn't all that used to handling something this big, having only been as far as the Four until a couple of weeks ago, but the size and heft of it seemed to suit his ample reach and fluid style. Bonging behind, it seemed, was very much becoming his forte.)

Finding Reverse Canterbury a relative walk in the park, Sally was able to let her focus shift away from the robotics of the method and onto Robert's ringing. Something about it seemed special, unique even. His long fifths was, of course, no longer than it ought to have been, and yet it *seemed* longer. It *felt* longer. It ran smoothly and evenly, without crashing, without bumping and with a steady, sturdy evenness that set her heart quite aflutter. It stayed there, out at the back, pounding away with the rhythmic predictability of a well-oiled metronome and it was all she could do to stay under it for four blows and not run out to embrace it in an impromptu, unsolicited dodge.

"This is all! Stand!" Derek smiled from ear to ear. His teaching was clearly paying dividends. Veronica had got round in one piece! As for her, she seemed to be in shock, as if aliens had seized control of her body, slotted her neatly into each gap as and when it appeared, and then vanished to the far reaches of the universe, their mission on Earth accomplished.

"So," said Robert to Sally, while Phyllis did a congratulatory circuit with the Quality Street, "shall we fix a date for the Cockshute? We might as well make hay while the sun shines."

"Let's not get ahead of ourselves. You can deal with my Bristols first."

"Royal? Maximus?"

"Oh, good Lord, no. I don't think I'll ever be a Bristol Maximus girl. I just want to move up from Minor to Major. Doesn't everybody?"

"Quite," agreed Robert.

Sally had suffered from Bristol paranoia ever since a nasty little man from Welshpool had muttered that she'd never go beyond Minor, but there was another side to her personality that would not let such slights affect her. Indeed, it spurred her on now, if anything, and she could see the path maybe even opening itself up eventually to Royal if she played her cards right.

"I guarantee we'll have your Bristols ship-shape and Bristol fashion before the year is out."

And they laughed together like old friends, like they had shared a whole lifetime of joy together. *He's so clever,* thought Sally, gazing up into his deep blue eyes. *How he managed to come up with that pun on the word 'Bristol', I've no idea. I would never have thought of that!* And she drifted off into musing as to whether there might be any possible pun that she could make in regard to Fanybedwell Surprise.

Later, after they had collectively failed to control some wayward Bastow, Clifford's Pleasure had come to nothing, but - on a positive note - Crispin had nailed his Queens, the evening drew to a close.

"Rounds and call changes," commanded Derek. "Who wants to call?"

"I'll do it," piped up Hazel. "In and out of Hagdyke?"

"Perfect," said Derek. "You can never have enough Hagdyke in my opinion."

"And do you want me to go down?" asked Hazel, looking at the clock, which said five to nine.

"Oh, yes, doesn't time fly! Better go down now or there'll be complaints!"

And off they went, tired but keen to bring the evening to a pleasing climax. The Hagdkye came off surprisingly well in the end and Hazel basked in the satisfying afterglow of a job well done.

"Look to the fall!" she called, and down they all went

with alacrity.

Before long, there came the final instruction to catch in Rounds. True to form, the ringers duly obliged by catching in something more akin to Exploding Tittums. Then they all put their coats on and descended the stairs in single file, chattering happily in self-congratulatory tones. All except Robert and Sally, that is.

"I need a bit of simulation," Sally had whispered to Robert just before the ringing down. "Let them all go and we can have the tower to ourselves. "Anything's better than Muriel's rhubarb wine and Wensleydale Unmentionables."

After they heard the church door clunk shut, they climbed the ladder, her leading him, this being, after all, her domain. Up amongst the bells, in the dim dusky half-light, she seized hold of the nearest clapper, pulled it towards her and shackled it to the lip. It held there, firm and solid, and Robert assured her with a smile that she could have done no better. But this was not all. She felt around the gudgeon to confirm that the bush had been adequately chamfered. Yes, it had. What about the castellated nuts? Yes, all present and correct. They had been well screwed and twinkled happily in full view. Finally, she took a moment to give the Ellacombe apparatus a quick wipe before checking the wheel, making sure that the flange was clear of debris and that the garter hole would allow for smooth and free passage. Everything was perfect. They were all set for a session of extensive, unfettered simulation.

The simulator whirred into life and Robert loaded up the first method. Sally pulled off. "It's too long!" she exclaimed.

"Stand!" said Robert with a tone of calm reassurance in his voice. "I'd been thinking this might be a bit too long for you. Don't worry. I've brought my fid." He whipped it out of his pocket with a flourish. It was shiny, perfectly smooth and made of steel.

"That's a nice one. Lucky you don't have to deal with Hazel's fid." Sally pointed to the foot-long wooden spike propped up in the corner next to the spare coils of rope and freshly-polished leather muffles. "Why on earth she needs something that big, I've no idea."

He gently eased his own sturdy fid through the twists of her rope and in no time he had taken it up to a more comfortable length.

"That's better," said Sally, trying a couple of quick blows. "Now, where were we?"

"Fanybedwell Surprise?" suggested Robert.

"I thought you'd never ask," she replied, huskily.

They went at it all night long. He introduced her to things she could never even have dreamed of: Cocking Alliance. Lovely Bottom Delight Minor. Cornish Knockers Surprise. Cuntastorp Delight Major. They ran the whole gamut and perfected the work at the bobs to boot. In and out, in and out, for hours. Only when the sun started rising behind Clittermoan Tea Hill, did they realise how long they had been at it and, after Robert had put her through her paces with a final short touch of Bristol, she let the limp tail end slip from her feverish, exhausted hands.

"Same time next week?" asked Robert, half-muffled, looking up at her and staring deep into her soul.

"I wouldn't miss it for the world..." replied Sally. She turned to slip away into the breaking dawn, when a sudden recollection stopped her in her tracks. "...unless," she continued, "they've got a special practice on at Church Stretton. In which case, I'll be going to that."

"But, Sally..." called Robert in desperation. "What about that Cockshute I was planning? I can't pull out now!"

"Robert, my sweet, you can count me in. It will be a delight."

"Single-hunt minor," he corrected her, pulling her

back for one final warm embrace. Incredulous that, at least for now, their pleasure had to be put on hold, he quietly whispered, "Is this all?"

"Till next time, my darling, this is all."

The End

...or is it?

Sally had never known a more perfect April day. The Cooktown orchids were in full bloom, opening their purple lips to the buttery sun, which peeked out from sheepish clouds onto the rolling Shropshire countryside. She had grabbed Cound. She had grabbed Worfield. She had even grabbed Chetton, having twisted the church warden's arm with a solemn promise to park with consideration. But now for the pièce de résistance: she was finally about to grab Willey!

Bob had promised that this would be a day to remember and Sally could detect a heightened sense of urgency in him. He was clearly keen that he should not let her down, and he had worked so hard on his composition, something that was clear for all to see. As far as Sally was concerned, he had nothing to fear: she had every confidence that his Cockshute would not disappoint...

Sally mused a while on that day, a day so wonderful that it even outshone the time that they had rung a peal of Bourne on the fourth of July. Everything had been perfect. And yet Sally's musings were tinged with an unignorable sadness. Grabbing Willey had been the last time that she was truly happy. Oh, how did she let her Bob slip away from her? And when, if ever, would she see him again...?

Find out in *Her First Long Length*, the eagerly anticipated international best-seller from Carbaretta Bartland, winner of the 2019 Verity Felcher Memorial Award for Campanological Erotica.

Printed in Great Britain
by Amazon

62366360R00017